BLINK

Amie McCracken

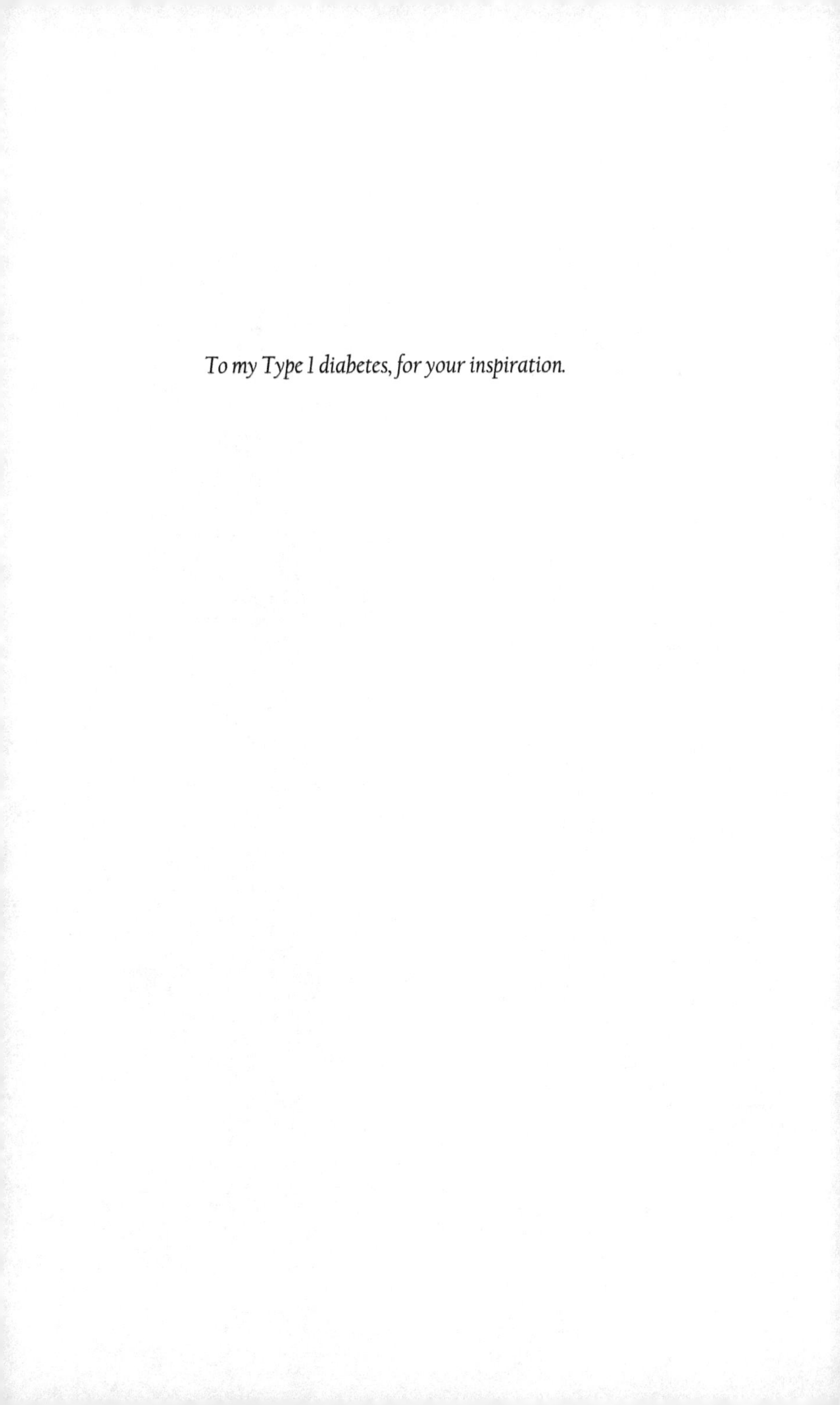

To my Type 1 diabetes, for your inspiration.

epilogue

Someone once told me you should always start at the end. So that's what I'm doing. This story begins where it concluded. At the moment I blinked, when I lost sight of the world and it lost sight of me. When all the bad things came crashing down upon me. When the sky fell.

I opened my eyes, and he was gone. My soul screamed. It wanted so badly to join him in that unknown place.

The cancer had eaten his body like a parasite. His cheeks were sunken; his torso, which no longer rose and fell with scattered, shallow breaths, had the consistency of putty and showed every rib; his legs which had once been so strong were just twigs. This man who could have been everything to me had left me to figure the rest of it out alone.

There are only so many blinks in life.

Don't think I don't know that. I've been reminded of it every hour of every day since I was a child. That feeling that if I do something wrong, make the tiniest mistake, relax into contentment a smidgen too long, those I love will blink no more.

I stood at the window, watching the sun peek over the horizon, and I remembered my task for the days ahead: to allow love. To let go. To give myself to others without worrying how I might hurt them, how I could cause disaster. It was going to be a hard road to follow, but I had told him I would try, and try I would.

chapter 1

The plane ride from London was long, the train ride wasn't, the car ride even shorter. I bounced up and down in my seat, ready for sand, sun, and ocean blue.

"Settle down, Piper," Daddy said.

"We'll be there soon enough, schatz," Mutti said. She smoothed my brown hair back and smiled. "Would you like to read me your book again?"

The back of the limo was dim, so Daddy turned on a light and they both listened while I read about Julie the gorilla. My own gorilla fell off the seat when the driver hit the brakes. I reached for him, pulling against my seatbelt.

"Mutti, please," I whined.

"Look outside," Daddy said. The window rolled down, and I saw the most beautiful gray-blue beach house ever. I squealed.

I unbuckled, grabbed Samson from the floor, and was out the door before the window was all the way back up. I stopped before the tall steps leading to the porch. The house was perfect. Exactly as Daddy had described it. This was his family's beach house in America, some place called Martha's Vineyard, though I didn't know who Martha was or where the vineyard was. There only seemed to be beach grass and a road.

The driver unloaded bags behind me. Daddy scooped me up and ran up the stairs, through the hallway, and onto the back porch.

"The ocean," I whispered.

"Let's leave Samson here so he doesn't get sandy," Daddy said.

"No! He wants to play too."

Daddy left Samson in my arms, and he ran down the steps and into the dunes where he set me down and took my hand.

We walked to the water, Daddy holding one hand and Samson the other. The sun was bright. It hurt my eyes, but I squinted and ignored it.

"Can we go swimming?"

"After we unpack, munchkin. We'll need suits, won't we?"

I giggled.

Daddy stopped at the line of wet sand. The sound of the ocean soothed me. Samson liked it too. I don't know how long we stood there, but soon I heard Mutti calling for us.

"Come on. We'll get suits and beach toys." Daddy put his hands under my arms and swung me around. The blue sky, gray ocean, tan sand, yellow beach grass all spun by.

Then we raced back to the house.

Not long after that, Mutti sat on a towel on the beach with Samson while I built a sand castle. Daddy came from the house with a basket and a big umbrella.

"The cook cut up some fruit. I've got cheese too. And wine," he said that last part out of the side of his mouth.

He wrestled with the umbrella, and I jumped up to rescue the basket from him. He sat down next to Mutti, breathing hard.

"I've won!"

"Good job," Mutti said and reached for the basket.

As we ate our food, I thought about how happy I was. Could anybody be this happy? Munching on watermelon, I pulled Samson into my lap for a cuddle and closed my eyes. The afternoon sun warmed my feet beyond the shade of the umbrella, the sweet juice dripped down my chin, and I sighed.

I felt Mutti's hand on my head and opened my eyes to smile at her. This was so nice.

*

The cook let me have a bite of the salmon on a cracker. She got right back to work and smiled when I begged for more.

"What are you drawing?" she asked, placing another cracker next to my markers. The kitchen was warm and smelled of lemons and thyme. The TV mumbled in the background.

"This is Samson on the beach with his family. They are building a jungle out of the sand. His little sister, Sarah, wants to use the rake to make a river, but Samson is using it to create vines lying on the jungle floor. His mother has told him to share, but he's being bad."

"Now why would he do that?" she asked. "Seems awfully rude."

"It is. He is feeling selfish. That's a new word I learned."

The cook leaned her chin in her hands to look at my picture. Then a timer went off and she ruffled my hair before going to the oven. On her way there, she turned up the TV.

Solid green covered the screen, eventually focusing into a jungle. I stopped drawing.

"This is the Congo," the reporter said. "Home to hundreds of creatures, but most famous for its gorillas."

"Look Samson," I cried and turned him to face the screen.

"Today, tragedy has struck. Researchers happened upon a very disturbing sight. What seems to have occurred this very afternoon is a massacre."

"While we were playing in the sand!" I said. "What's a massacre?" But the cook wasn't paying attention and Samson wouldn't answer because his eyes were glued to the TV.

"These images might be disturbing for younger viewers. Primatologists call it the largest poaching event to date. This family of gorillas was slaughtered for profit. Their babies stolen to be sold. Their body parts hacked and maimed."

The reporter kept talking but his voice faded. Bloody gorilla arms, gorilla faces with teeth torn out, mountains of gorilla stacked and left.

I screamed.

The cook whipped around with a hot dish of green beans, and they went flying. She looked from me to the TV and screamed herself.

I jumped from my stool and dashed into the sunroom where my parents stood, their wine glasses spilled across the floor.

"Daddy!" I flew into his arms.

Daddy's shirt muffled the sound, but I heard Mutti whisper, "What happened?"

"It's all my fault. They died when I was happy. I killed all of them," I screamed. My body felt cold.

"You're shivering, schatz," Mutti said, her hand on my back. "Who died?"

"The gorillas! All of them!"

I broke from Daddy's arms and punched Mutti's hand away. I saw the porch door open and ran. Down the stairs, through the dunes, across the sand.

Someone followed me, cried out for me to stop. But I couldn't. My chest was on fire; my eyes leaked so many tears, it hurt.

I ran right into the water. It cooled the pain. Large arms scooped me up, and the smell of Daddy took over the smell of salt and sun. He carried me back to the house where they undressed me and wrapped me in a blanket. Mutti handed me Samson and cradled me on the big sofa. I heard the cook talking with Daddy, but I couldn't understand.

"It's my fault," I whispered. "My fault. I was selfish. My fault."

"Nein," Mutti said. "No, my love. Why would you ever think that?"

I sat up and looked at her, Samson falling to the floor, forgotten.

"Don't you understand? When I was happiest, when I closed my eyes to enjoy the sun, that's when my friends were killed. Massacre. I caused the massacre because I was selfish."

Mutti's face was gray. I put a hand on her cheek.

"I can never let that happen again," I said.

*

Daddy carried me upstairs and put me in a warm bath. Mutti washed me with her silky hands while singing some of our German lullabies. I stood out of the water and stepped into a big towel. The world felt safe and soft until I remembered my friends. I started to shake and shiver again, images of monkey parts lying on the floor in front of me. A scream gurgled up from my chest and out my mouth.

"Louis!" Mutti called. Her arms were around me, but I wanted free. Free to run from the blood on the floor.

Daddy ran into the room and knelt down with us. He didn't grab me; he put his hands on my face and whispered words. The blood on the tile turned back to water and the world felt soft and safe again. Mutti was crying. They took me to their bed and lay on either side of me. Sounds of the ocean and wind and seagulls came through the propped French doors. Another of Mutti's lullabies helped me fall asleep.

Mutti's voice filled the dark room. She sang like an angel. Daddy had Samson and he tucked him in between us. If my heart wasn't broken and bleeding, if Samson's family had been safe in the jungle, if I hadn't caused such a massacre...

I fell asleep with Mutti's lullaby in my ears and gorillas rolling in the grass before my eyes.

Something jostled me awake. Daddy's arm reaching across to touch Mutti. She cried into a pillow. My eyes slid shut, but their voices drifted in the air around me.

"It's simply a traumatic event," Daddy said. "We've

always known she's overly empathetic. Her belief that her happiness causes catastrophic events is just her way of expressing pain."

"But isn't it strange that she makes these connections?" Mutti whispered and then sniffled.

"When was the last time?"

"The housekeeper's mother fell ill a few months ago. Piper told me she had been so excited to get an A on her German spelling test and she went to tell Judy, who was crying and packing to leave."

"Piper blamed herself?"

"Of course."

The room shook with their silence. The sound of the waves crashing on the beach was so powerful I thought we would get wet.

"It's always been like this," Mutti said.

"Don't do that. Don't give it power. That's nonsense."

"Even when she was a baby. Chaos around her when she's happy. Her first laugh. Don't you remember?"

Daddy didn't answer. I was so tired, but I wanted to hear what had happened. Like climbing through mud, I tried to wake up. But I couldn't. Sleep won. And I didn't wake again until the morning, the sun streaming in and my parents sleeping on either side of me, their hands linked above my head.

*

It wasn't the way the climbing wall wobbled when I was halfway up. Nor was it the ringing in my ear that felt like a very loud whistle inches from my face. Or the fact that I couldn't breathe even though I hadn't been running. It was the way my hands shook. Especially when I pulled one away from the wall to see it shiver uncontrollably. The other simply couldn't hold on and I began to fall, but I don't remember hitting the ground.

I do remember the beeping that replaced the ringing; the smell of sickness and bleach; the pounding in my head. When I opened my eyes, the headache intensified. I closed them again.

"Mutti?" I asked.

"Right here, schatzi," she said. The croak of her slight German accent made me burst into tears.

"Oh liebling, everything is fine. You must be so scared. The doctor will explain in just a moment."

Her cool and creamy hands touched my face. It lessened the headache.

"What happened? Where are we?"

"You fell at school. You passed out. But you're just fine... well, nothing broken...well, nothing from the fall."

My eyes popped open. "What do you mean!"

A nurse ran in to restrain me while I thrashed on the bed. Mutti's hands were gentle but firm. One of my flailing arms connected with her cheek. Skin meeting skin, muscle scraping teeth, a gasp and a sudden stop. We all froze.

"The doctor will be in shortly," the nurse said as she set my bed to rights and made sure I hadn't disconnected my IV.

The doctor was in shortly, along with Daddy. He came over to sit on my bed and hold my hand. The doctor took the tablet with my chart and tucked it under his arm.

"Good news first as it's simpler," he said. Mutti smiled at him. I looked at her, at Daddy, at Mutti, at the doctor, at Daddy.

"You fell from the climbing wall but didn't hurt your-self. A few bruises. The reason you fell is why you're in the hospital. Piper, you passed out. You lost conscious-ness because your blood sugar was very high for a very long time."

"What does that mean?" I whispered to Daddy. "I ate too many sweets? I didn't have any at lunch."

"You have Type 1 diabetes," the doctor continued. "It can happen at any age. You didn't do anything to cause it. We don't really know what causes it. But we can teach you how to manage it. It's something you'll have the rest of your life."

He pulled the tablet out and swiped through it. Then he handed it to Daddy.

"There are some videos on there. I'll let you talk to her for a bit before we send the educator in."

"Thank you," Daddy said and took the tablet.

*

I recall one day when my class went to the aquarium. We were allowed to wander through the last few rooms alone as long as we didn't talk. With all that silence and hum of fish tanks, some of us burst into giggles. But I stopped to watch the jellyfish through a circular window. The sounds in the room faded away—titters, bubbles, mechanical shushing. I felt the water of the tank filling my ears, the salt stinging my eyes. The jellyfish surrounded me but didn't touch me. We simply floated in harmony, the world disappearing in the background and leaving us be.

As I sat in my hospital bed that day, my parents' voices washing over me, I remembered those jellyfish. But the serenity didn't last long.

"Piper?" Daddy said. "We don't need to bombard you with everything today."

"We want to be sure you're okay," Mutti said. Tears glistened on her cheeks but she smiled. "Everything is going to be okay."

"You keep saying that," I said. "It's obviously not. I'm sick. And I will be forever now."

They looked at each other.

"Yes," Daddy said, pausing. "But it's doable. It's not something to let take over your life. I read some articles and watched videos and started a book."

I finally saw the dark circles under his eyes, the stubble on his chin, the fact that he was still wearing a crumpled suit.

"Have a look at this video and we'll talk about it more."

They left me alone in the room. The video was a collection of diabetics saying they could do anything they wanted. I still had no idea what was wrong with my body, but apparently I could go mountain biking or travel to Timbuktu if I wanted.

I set the tablet on the bedside table and rolled away from the door to curl up under the blankets.

Soon after, I still hadn't fallen asleep, but I heard the squeak of shoes on the floor and the groan of the leather visitor's chair behind me. Someone tapped and clicked on a tablet. The video I had watched started over again.

"Piper?" a voice I didn't recognize asked. But it sounded like lazy Sunday mornings with bowls of hot chocolate and crossword puzzles with Daddy.

I grunted.

"Do you know why you're in the hospital? A simple grunt for yes, two for no please."

I grunted twice.

"You fell on the playground because you have Diabetic Ketoacidosis. Big words meaning you have too much sugar in your body."

"I already told Daddy I hadn't had any sweets." I sat up and faced the stranger.

"Hello Piper." She smiled. That smile was the rest of Sunday—lying in the hammock reading, playing tag with Fluffy, watching a movie in German with Mutti.

I smiled back.

"No. Your body decided to attack itself and now part of you doesn't work. But it's okay because we can manually control your blood sugar. With medicine."

"What part of me is broken?"

"Before we get into all that, I'm Layla. It's nice to meet you." She held out a hand for me to shake. I hesitated and then set my own hand inside hers. Like an electric shock, I felt instantly that she was on my side. Things might be okay, but I still wasn't happy.

Layla spent the afternoon and well into the evening explaining Type 1 diabetes to me, my new life-long companion.

*

"Hello, schatz. How are you feeling?" Mutti came in with a glass of water for me. My brain felt fuzzy and overloaded. But a sleepy smile crept onto my face.

"Better."

"I'm so glad. Daddy and I are here for you no matter what. It's okay if you get mad." She settled on the edge of my bed.

"I'm a little mad, but Layla explained a lot. I think I understand."

Mutti lay down next to me and held my hand. We watched the artificial light come through the window to play on the ceiling. London was always alive. It didn't matter how sleepy I was. That was part of why I loved this city; because someone was always awake. The world could be on fire while I was lost in a magical castle, and someone would take care of it. I never had to worry; I was always safe as long as London's lights were on.

Mutti and Daddy drove home that night from Evelina London Children's Hospital to our home in Windsor. They promised to pick up a few things for me, and I was happy to see them go as they needed new clothes and a good night's sleep.

The next morning, I woke with the sunshine. The nurse was checking everything, her hand on my arm.

"Didn't mean to wake you, love. Go back to sleep for a bit."

"Can I have breakfast?"

"You're hungry? Why, of course. Let me get the doctor for a blood sugar test and insulin dosage."

She left and I wiggled upward in the bed, trying not to put pressure on my IV hand. It hurt. The sunshine felt like a warm bath, and I leaned into the starched pillow, the smell of cleanliness filling my head. I sighed and just before I closed my eyes in contentment, I saw the digital clock across the room click to exactly seven a.m.

A few minutes later, the doctor came in.

"Let's try this," he said. He handed me a machine the size of a small mobile phone in a bag with a cylinder and a container of strips of plastic.

"These are test strips. This is the glucose monitor. This is the poker." He picked up the cylinder and pulled back a cocking mechanism then pushed a button. It popped, loudly, and I jumped.

"It'll poke you with a tiny needle. It won't hurt. This is how you put the strip in."

He inserted the strip in the machine, cocked the cylinder, grabbed my hand, put the cylinder up to my finger, and hit the button. I screamed.

He shoved my arm closer to the strip and a blood bead on the end of my finger was sucked up into it. He pushed a cotton swab to my throbbing finger with a lot of force, only making it worse, and looked at his watch.

"This number is okay. You'll be eating a specific amount of carbohydrates and you have automatic insulin for now. We'll get to injections tomorrow. You'll need to give yourself an injection of insulin every time you eat something."

I gulped.

Then he left.

I cradled my hand and watched my tears fall to the crinkly blanket.

The scuffle of shoes alerted me to another presence.

"I hope it's Mutti," I whispered to myself but didn't look up. Purple tennis shoes came into my vision, lining up perfectly next to my bed.

"Dear Piper. Why are you crying?" The sound of her voice was ice to my sore finger.

She gently pulled my hand out of the cage I had created with my body. She kissed it.

"It hurts," I said.

"Soon it won't. I've brought your breakfast. Do you want to eat?"

"I want my mum."

"How about you start on this lovely fruit salad and I'll go find her."

"She's not been here yet."

"Really? Maybe they hit traffic. I'll go speak with the nurse."

She held out a fork to me. I finally lifted my head and saw the food tray. My stomach rumbled. With the fork safely in my hands, Layla left the room.

*

I finished everything on my plate as the doctor had instructed, but I was still hungry. It was already nine a.m. and Mutti still hadn't come.

The room seemed to get bigger and colder with each flip of the digital clock numbers. I pulled the sheet around my shoulders and started humming one of Mutti's lullabies. Someone down the hall moaned. Machines in the other rooms beeped and whirred. Each set of shoes that squeaked by my door had me flicking my eyes away from the clock in anticipation.

Finally, finally, Layla came with a nurse. They sat down on either side of me after moving the tray of dishes. Layla took my hand.

"My darling Piper..."

Her voice faded. My ears blocked with cotton. I knew I shouldn't have let myself feel that moment of contentment upon waking. It was all my fault. Again.

Now the room shrank. It closed in on me, filling with water that trickled in at first then gushed through the broken windows to envelop my nose and mouth.

They were dead. At precisely seven a.m. that morning, an out-of-control lorry shoved their car through the barrier of Lambeth Bridge, and they drowned in the River Thames. Because of me.

I wailed. I thrashed. I tore the sheets and ripped the IV from my hand. No sound came to my ears for they were already drowning in water. But soon the nurse stabbed me with a needle and my energy waned. I lay still, whimpering.

chapter 2

"Piper, I don't understand. You ran away to Germany to get away, to find yourself. Now, two years later, you're coming back?" Layla said. Her voice still soothed like a cup of warm tea, even over the phone, even nine years later. She had never abandoned me. Through the hell of living with one of my parents' high-executive, forever-single, never-planned-for-children-let-alone-a-sick one British friends. A person I hadn't really known but who had custody over me, and my trust fund, until I turned eighteen, considering any American family on my dad's side and any German family on my mother's side were long gone. Through my intense need to keep my diabetes and my life under control. Through my wild escape to my mother's homeland. Layla had always been there.

"Is two years not enough to find myself?" I asked. I paced my tiny room and threw things into piles for packing, throwing out, and posting. There wasn't much to take with me.

"It's plenty. But why don't you want to stay?"

"Berlin is cool. Really. But it's not home. I can't settle. That's probably good, but I miss London. And you," I said.

That and maybe one fling too many had made me feel rest-less. Sebastian had been a good friend, and so far, I hadn't ruined things for him. I didn't want that to change. I put the phone on speaker and set it down on the floor where I sat to rifle through a stack of papers.

"Your blood sugars are still good?"

"Yes Mother."

"Don't do that. I may be your friend, but first I am your doctor. I didn't go through medical school for the plaque on my wall. And since you refused to find a doctor in Berlin, I have to keep up on you."

"You know I don't need a doctor. I have you. Plus, I switched from injections to an insulin pump ages ago, so I have better control. And you get downloads directly from that in my monthly email. Stop fretting." I looked out the window to find sunshine peeking through the clouds. "I'll call you later. The sun came out. Gotta go running."

"When does your plane—"

I hung up on her. Though I loved her, I didn't want her picking me up at the airport. If I let her much closer to my heart and relaxed for one tiny moment... I couldn't bear to think what would happen if she got hurt because I was happy with life. So I didn't allow contentment, and I didn't let Layla in further than she already was.

Two days later I let my rucksack tumble to the grass on the Southbank under London's Eye. One of my favorite places, one of the last places I remember being with my parents before the hospital. I had been so afraid to ride it. But Daddy pushed; he made me. By the time we reached the pinnacle, I no longer remembered the fear—lost in the beauty of my city skyline.

Even from the park below it, bathing in golden sunshine, I pictured exactly how London looked from above. Glass and metal winking at me, stone absorbing the sunshine. The Gherkin and Shard standing proud above the older buildings like Westminster Abbey and St. Paul's Cathedral.

My phone rang.

It was a number I didn't know.

"Hello?"

"Piper Ainsley?"

"Yes, who is this?"

"I finally found you," a very gentlemanly sounding gentleman said.

"Can I help you?" I peered up at the Eye, circling slowly, shading my eyes from the glare with my hand.

"I'm Rebecca Worthy's solicitor."

I gasped and coughed on my own saliva.

"Are you all right?" he asked.

"Is Rebecca okay?"

"Yes, well, sort of. Your guardian has gotten herself in a bit of trouble—"

"Is she alive? And she's no longer my guardian."

He coughed. "She's alive. Since you weren't available to sign the paperwork at the age of eighteen, she still has partial control of your trust. And, well," he paused.

I stood up to pace through the crowd of school children and tourists before me. "Go on," I said.

"She committed tax fraud. To pay the fines she ran out of money and then used part of your trust."

"Excuse me?" I screamed. "Das ist total scheisse!" I slipped into German. I'd been using it for two years; it came naturally.

"Can you come in and sign the paperwork now?"

"I'll be there in twenty minutes."

I hung up without realizing I had no idea where to go. A text arrived with an address. Before striding to the Tube with all my pent up anger, I paused to test my blood sugar. It was perfect, as I knew it would be, so I set out to find what state my finances were in.

*

A total shambles, that's what my trust was, but at least I was finally, solely in control. I walked, with my large rucksack, from the solicitor's office all the way to a flat in East London where I had an appointment to view. I needed to blow off steam. The walk took over an hour. And I had to stop to treat a low blood sugar. But it kept my anger at a manageable level.

The flat was in an old building with the ground floor empty and vandalized. All along the street stood barber-shops and men's fashion stores. I saw a pop-up shop with art made of vinyl records at the end of the street. Across from the entrance to the flat was a pub: The Horse and Hound. I vowed that would be my first stop after signing the lease and getting my keys.

And it was exactly where I ended up after signing for the flat. With high ceilings, brick walls, floor-to-ceiling windows, a hot-plate and mini fridge, and a shared bathroom down the hall, I couldn't not rent it. Plus, it fit perfectly in my new budget.

I lifted my glass of cider and sipped.

"Can I get you anything else?" the barman asked. He had come over to wipe my table down.

"Nah, thanks."

He sat down.

I sat up.

"You just look like you need something more."

I instantly reached for my glucose monitor, thinking he meant I looked pale or strange. I poked my finger under cover of the table. Everything was under control.

"What do you mean?" I asked.

His deep brown eyes sparkled, and I took in his creamy chocolate skin and stupid grin. Probably in his early twenties, he was skinny but had a rugged face. *Yummy* is what came to mind. I wiped the condensation from my glass.

"How about you wait here until I finish my shift and we'll go to dinner together?"

The pub was suddenly quiet, like someone had turned down the volume. My heart skipped in an I-want-to-escape way.

"Sorry but I have a lot to do tonight." I waved at my rucksack in explanation and looked deep into my golden drink.

"Tomorrow?"

My new pub, the place nearest my new flat, was quickly becoming a pain in the ass.

"Maybe," I said and downed the rest of my cider. Then I stood before he spoke again and left to find a hostel for the night. Tomorrow I would have a bed sent to the flat and I'd be able to sleep in a place that was my own.

*

The state of my finances didn't leave me destitute, but I thought it prudent to find a job. I got up the next morning with that as my goal for the day. First I went running in an unkempt park nearby.

Breathing heavily, sweat tickling my inner arms, I paused by a bench and a closed iron gate. Through the gate, I saw the wild green overpowering what looked like gravestones.

"It's an old cemetery," a man behind me said. I turned to see his portly self, leaning on a broom with a rubbish bag by his side.

"Why would they leave the graves in a park?"

"Don't know. I just keep it clean."

Very suddenly the world tilted and I stumbled, my hand planting firmly on a cold stone angel next to the gate.

"You okay, miss?" His hand grasped my elbow.

"I'm diabetic. If I pass out, just know that."

He led me to a bench where I fumbled in my crossover for my test kit and sugar. My tongue went numb. My fingers tingled. The sidewalk in front of me glinted and shone even though the trees blocked all sunlight.

Next I knew, I was staring up at the inside of an ambulance—the white ceiling, the shelves of machinery, and the kind smiling face of an old man.

"Who are you?" I mumbled.

"I called 999. Told 'em you were diabetic. Thought that might be a good idea seeing as you were rambling on about diamonds in the sidewalk."

"Thank you," I said and closed my eyes again.

The voice of someone I knew, one dipped in chocolate and sprinkles, was what I heard next. But though it soothed me, it did not sound happy.

Layla.

"I cannot believe this. You've had her here since this morning and not told me? I'm her emergency contact. Besides being her physician. Let me in!"

I propped myself on my elbows. A large nurse stood in the doorway, blocking Layla.

"Let her in," I called.

"You're awake!" they both said.

I vomited the contents of my stomach over the bed, the wave cascading to the floor. The horrific, chunky splash and the acidic smell made me heave again. The nurse ran to clean up, and Layla grabbed paper towels to wipe me down.

"Sorry, so sorry," I mumbled.

"Love. Don't apologize."

The smell eventually masked by lemons and bleach, and supplied with fresh bed linens and a robe, I lay back with sweaty palms and the shakes. If I was hoping to get my life back on track, it wasn't really working.

"This is not what I want to see, Piper," Layla said.

"I said sorry."

"That's not what I want either. I can't control you, and we both know that, but I won't lose you. What can we do to make this better? I've had them run your A1c and it's fine. Will you email me your blood sugars?"

"I was running. An old man helped me."

"Did you not test before?"

"I found a flat. I'm looking for a job too."

"Will this forever be a one-sided conversation?"

"It's in East London. Very chic."

"Fine. When can I come over for dinner?"

"I don't have much of a kitchen, but there are tons of pubs. How about you take me home when they let me out this afternoon?"

"Good. You can show me your blood sugars then."

I didn't answer her. I lay back and let the shakes take me to another world. One where my surroundings vibrated and I held still.

*

While Layla hadn't thought it funny when I announced she was not only taking me home but helping me move in, she couldn't keep from smiling when we got inside. I'd had the bed delivered and we got to work putting it together after ordering Japanese rice bowl take-out. I spent the evening chattering with her, obediently showing her my meticulous blood sugar charts, and enjoying her company.

But, and there's always a but, I wasn't happy. My mind was on hospitals and potential jobs and how I could make myself better. It was time to change my routine a tiny bit.

"Layla."

"Yes?" She focused on turning a stubborn screw.

"Could I borrow some money?"

"Whatever for?"

Practical Layla.

"I need something new. I was thinking a personal trainer. And the solicitor says I should get a settlement of some sort so I can pay you back."

"You can't run in the park anymore?" She giggled. "I thought you were getting a job?"

I took a bite of veg and rice from the carton.

"I am. But I need something new."

"Moving back isn't new? Never mind. I will gladly start a class with you or join a book club, but you are in great shape and can keep yourself that way without paying a trainer. Find a better use for your money."

She swiped my empty plate from me and started piling all the trash in a bag. She kissed my cheek and lugged the bag out the door.

*

"Well, um, you have no experience?"

The sales guy's bright cheery voice turning a statement into a question, did nothing for lessening the blow. Shop after shop said the same thing. I was continually sinking deeper. The sunlight no longer filtered through the murky water. My lungs had gone beyond burning and now couldn't muster the energy to ask for air.

"No," I said. I left my scant resume in his hands and turned to go. London, a city full of opportunity, for those already getting a hand up.

On the walk home, I tested my blood sugar. High. High enough that I didn't feel well. Incredibly thirsty in fact. And of course, in front of my face was The Horse and Hound. The barman from the other night, standing in the window and hanging a *Help Wanted* sign, waved me in. I could really use a glass of water, and a distraction.

My blood sugar result had sent my blood pressure skyrocketing to meet. Now I wasn't just depressed, I was also angry. I thought back over my day to pinpoint the culprit for this high—an incorrect calculation, too much stress, a snack I hadn't accounted for, too little water—probably all. Too many uncontrollable factors. I gave myself insulin.

The barman was still in the window, making funny faces at me while I stood on the sidewalk in my own little diabetic world. I ducked my head to hide my smile and stepped inside.

"Hiya!" he bounced into my path.

"Hi?"

"What can I get ya?"

"Water please."

"Coming right up."

I went to one of the big, brown leather sofas ensconcing the window. When I turned to sit, I saw the barman by the kitchen door, bent in half, coughing violently. I looked away in shame. The function of his body was not something to gawk at. He came back with two glasses and sat next to me, propping his feet on the coffee table. He was short of breath but still smiling.

"You didn't come back," he said.

"I'm back now." I glanced around to ensure our privacy, but the place was dead. "Are you all right?" I whispered.

"What? Oh, yeah. No worries." He flung a hand at me. "I'm Trey, by the way."

"Piper." We shook. I downed my water then grabbed the second glass.

"Thirsty?" His eyebrow rose. "I'm gonna have my lunch. What do you want?"

"A salad?"

"Really?" He eyed me up and down. "I think you need a pasty."

"No!" I shouted, then slapped my hand over my mouth. "I'm so sorry. I can't have the carbohydrates."

"One of those?" He rolled his eyes. I felt the gap between our thighs on the sofa widening. It became a canyon, flooded with a raging river, and had me yelling across to no avail. Instead of bothering to explain, I shrugged. Trey mimicked me and took the empty glasses with him.

He came back with two scrumptious salads which I accepted graciously. Then I laughed.

"Please tell me you're eating one of these?"

He also laughed and plonked down.

"Yes. While I do eat carbs, I've also been upping my vitamins and greens."

Through a giant bite of spinach, I mumbled, "Any particular reason?"

My cheeks must have flashed crimson before I swallowed and repeated myself.

"Let's not get into that. How about we talk about where we're going for dinner instead?"

I giggled. Then I shoved the schoolgirl back into her closet and remembered who I really was. One little blip of happiness and all of Germany could go up in smoke.

"Actually, I wanted to ask about the job here."

"Oh?" Trey said and sipped his water.

"Thing is, well, I have no experience." My lap was suddenly very interesting. Especially when I noticed the rogue dollop of salad dressing running down my thigh.

"Not a prob. I'll get you an app. Then we can talk about that date." He winked and walked off again.

I stuffed the salad down and gathered my things. As he walked up, I was giving insulin with my pump.

"Piper. Will you ever forgive me? I feel like a right ass now. You're diabetic?"

"How did you know?"

"I have a friend of a friend who has a pump like yours. He explained it all to me once. The carbs..."

The application dangled from his limp hand. I snatched it and booked it to the door.

"No biggie. Thanks!" I called and breathed deeply of the pollution congested air outside.

chapter 3

The morning air did its job. I was awake and jazzed for my run. And it was important that this day start well, since I was due for my first attempt at earning my own money at The Horse and Hound that afternoon.

My blood sugar was perfect when I tested in the entrance to my building, so I tucked the monitor back in my pouch and took off toward the park.

This time the iron gate was open. I wended my way along the nearly overgrown and shaded paths, admiring the crumbling gravestones and the cool, damp earth smells.

Out the other side and back around to the pond, I slowed to a walk by a coffee stand. I saw the old caretaker who had called an ambulance for me, sweeping the sidewalk. So I bought two coffees and two pastries.

When I held one out to him, he smiled.

"I'm Piper."

"Nice to finally meet you. I'm Joe."

"Will you sit with me?" I shrugged toward a bench and then sat. "I need to say thank you. You saved my life."

Joe grunted and sat. "It was the least I could do."

He watched as I pricked my finger, silently questioned me with his bushy eyebrows, and tucked in after I nodded.

"Do you like your job?" I asked after a bite of my plain croissant.

"I get to be outdoors."

We sat in camaraderie for a moment.

"I start my first job today," I said. The croissant now sat in my lap. I was suddenly very unhungry. But I had to eat it because I had given insulin, and without the sugar from the food I would again go dangerously low. I didn't need another trip to the hospital.

"There will be more," he said.

I sipped my coffee and figured he was right. The nerves were unnecessary.

"Thanks for the thank you," he said and went back to his sweeping. I watched his methodical movements and zoned out while finishing my snack.

Then I power-walked home to agonize over my outfit and hairdo.

*

What I hadn't thought about was practicality. A barmaid needs comfortable shoes—the only two pairs I own both are. But I hadn't counted on the sticky floors. Neither had I thought to pull my hair out of my face. No one cared what I looked like as long as I delivered their food and drink and gave correct change. After dipping my styled locks in one too many pints, I used a twist tie to put it up. Trey tugged on my pony as he walked by and laughed at me. And after the hundredth time of wiping sloshed beer on my nice black trousers, Trey whipped me with a bar towel and then tucked it in my apron.

By the end of the night I felt dead, and yet, so alive. The bar was quiet. We only had to clean up. Trey ran by one last time and tapped one shoulder as he ran around to the other. I laughed with him.

"How'd it go, newbie?"

"Not bad." I leaned on the counter. "Not bad at all."

Suddenly, a coughing fit took Trey to his knees. I put a hand on his back and looked around for help.

"I'm fine," he said. He hawked something into his bar towel and wiped his face, immediately tossing the rag into the laundry below the counter.

"Are you sure?"

"Most definitely. But I'd be even better if I could put 'dinner with Piper' in my schedule."

I scoffed.

Then after another minute of staring at each other, I blurted, "Okay."

*

My bed was no comfort that night. Happiness glowed around me like some horrible night light coming from my pores. My eye twitched. My body wouldn't stop shaking. I stood on a precipice. I knew something bad was on its way. It had to be. How could I have let my guard down?

Sleep a distant dream, I jumped from bed and pulled out my blank postcards—a collection of places visited but notes never sent to people I couldn't love. The process of lining them on my wall was like counting sheep. Though I still got no sleep, I was at least calmed by the monotony.

I woke with a postcard plastered to my cheek and my body contorted into a pretzel on the wood floor. A few snaps and pops of joints and tendons and I was standing.

The only thing to do was run. Run off the exhaustion; run off the fear; run to gain momentum and control. This time I took a more circuitous route and didn't reach the park until I was already drenched in sweat. My blood sugars remained steady, and I made a mental note to show Layla that fact when I saw her the next day.

I saw Joe with his back to me up ahead, and I slowed to a jog. I tapped his shoulder and prepared a big smile. But the face that turned to me wasn't Joe.

"Hello," he said. "What can I do for you, pretty lady?" He sidled closer; I inched away.

"I thought you were someone else. Sorry." I turned to leave until he said more. It stopped me in my tracks.

"Joe? We get mistaken all the time. Silly, seeing as I'm taller. Anyways, won't happen anymore. He's been fired."

"What?" I spun around.

"Some issue with kids getting in the supply cabinet or something. Too bad that. He loved this job. He'll be hard pressed to find something else."

A blur of green. Some brown. A bit of blue. Red and orange here and there. Color was all I took in as I raced away, tears making rivulets in my cheeks and threatening to erode me away.

I had known. I had known, and I had let it happen. When would I ever learn?

chapter 4

Layla dragged me to a bookshop near Trafalgar Square. I hadn't been to central London since being back and memories swept over me like fog.

We stepped out of Layla's taxi and into the throngs. The screens advertising musicals and plays threw me back to a few times my parents had brought me and a few times I had been left home so they could partake. I let Layla lead me by the hand until the shop shrouded us in hushed whispers. She wanted me to do the book club thing and made a bee-line for the selection. I halted in my tracks because a very familiar form stood before the shelves.

Trey.

I hunted for cover but found none before Layla called across the store for me. Trey lifted his nose from a book and smiled.

"Hello, Piper," he said as I came up beside Layla.

"Who's your friend?" Layla asked. Her eyes glinted with mischievous plans to wed me to this fine young gentleman then and there.

"We work together." I shut her down. "Trey this is my doctor," I said. They both looked like drenched puppies.

"Did you find the book we need?" I asked Layla.

"Yes," she grumbled.

"What book?" Trey asked and leaned over. "That's a good one. But it helps to have the visual before you read it. Tower Bridge features heavily in the main character's fears. I used to do the tours there and can get us in for free. Fancy a trip?" Trey said.

Layla practically jumped up and down while I shook my head.

"Come on. It's the perfect day-off distraction. You'll enjoy your novel even more if you can feel the atmosphere of standing on thin air."

This time Trey dragged me through the streets and into the underground; Layla tagging along.

Before I knew it, the view between my feet should have been breathtaking but it was only nauseating. A tiny fracture and I could either splat on the road or in the water. Worst case scenario, I hit the bridge on the way into the river. Best case scenario—not be here at all. I desperately wanted to test my blood sugar but couldn't unglue my hands from the railing.

Layla was in her own personal heaven—a private tour. She kept looking past him to wink at me, or wiggle her eyebrows, or any other manner of approval for his suitableness that she thought he couldn't see though she stood facing him.

"We're forty-two meters above the river now. The bridge was a modern marvel in the late 1800s with its steam-driven, bascule-raising machinery. That was replaced in 1976 by electric motors," Trey said, gesturing here and there. "The character spends time in this walkway contemplating death—"

"No wonder," I interrupted.

Trey laughed. "It's plenty sturdy." He stamped his foot in the middle of a pane of glass.

I trembled, feeling the gush of air as the pane broke beneath us and we were swept into nothingness. The fall was slow and agonizing, leaving time for my entire life to play before my eyes. When I finally opened them to face my death head on, I realized I was still on the glass bridge with a group of Chinese tourists squeezing past me.

We reached the opposite side and finished the tour.

Trey left us in the engine rooms, saying he had an appointment. He casually mentioned our date as well. As Layla started through the museum, she plugged her arm through mine and gushed like a little girl.

"A date?" she said.

We stood before a giant steam engine part. The metal and informational placards felt as far from the topic of conversation as could be, more like my heart, all cold and hard and logical.

"I've been on dates before. This is more of a friend thing." I moved on to the next panel.

"That didn't sound like a casual thing. He likes you." She nudged me.

"He's confused." I wandered into the next room, Layla still attached to my arm. She wasn't even reading the facts, then again, neither was I.

"I think you're the one who is confused. But have it your way. You'll see once you've spent more time with him.

I can already tell that he's wonderful." She left me and stepped into a lift. I stayed behind for the next one. If I stood him up Layla would kill me, and she might even find out because she and Trey had exchanged phone numbers.

I would have to go through with it now, tragedy magic or no. It was only dinner after all, what harm could it do?

*

I met Trey at The Horse and Hound. My clothing choice and hair up-do had been significantly simpler that my first night of work—a skirt and sweater, an easy but messy bun. I didn't even feel the need to test my blood sugar in a fit of anxiety. Everything was prim and proper and this was just dinner with a friend. Or so I thought/hoped.

When he came bouncing up—honestly looking incredibly sexy in a button down and jeans—I noticed a bag in his hands. He pulled out a salad in a plastic container and handed it to me.

"It's customary to give plants to a girl, but I think you're confused on the type of plants," I said. The salad bowl hung heavy from my hand. Trey laughed.

"That's dinner. We have somewhere to be and they serve drinks but not dinner."

"This is not exactly to-go food."

"You doubt me?" Trey winked. He snatched the salad back and led me to my familiar park where we sat and ate.

"I wanted carb free, but I make no promises for dessert." He winked again. I snorted through my mouthful of rocket and spinach.

"Thoughtful, thanks," I said and tipped my fork to him. "There are other options, though." I wanted to slap myself as soon as the words jumped from my mouth. "This is great." I attempted recovery but felt a failure.

Trey munched his rabbit food. After another few awkward moments, I spoke again.

"How was your appointment the other day?"

It seemed I was only digging a further hole. Trey's face clouded over.

"Just a doctor," he said.

I didn't press.

"Where are we going?" I asked.

"You'll see." That was all I got until we finished eating and he popped up, one hand out to accept mine.

The sun set while we walked. And though Trey hinted at urgency, we didn't hop onto a bus. The buildings washed with gold and then purple. The people turned from mums and kids to businessmen, then to those in fancier dress and a giddy hop to their step.

"Here we are." Trey turned sharply into a dark doorway with no indication of style.

Inside was a rather bland and blank room, dimly lit with small bar-height tables and a few sofas lining the wall. The crowd also gave me no indication as they were bedecked in things ranging from Sunday sweats to little black dresses.

Trey ordered us some psychedelic neon drinks and took me to a table. I silently gave thanks that he hadn't chosen a sofa to avoid any possible cuddling.

Stashed in my own personal space atop a spinning barstool, I waited.

The door slammed shut, the lights switched off, and I grabbed our table for balance. Trey's hand—I hoped it was Trey's—landed on top of mine.

"What the—"

Loud acoustic guitar cut off the rest of my question and a sweet voice, the crackle of a record coming through the speakers. Simon and Garfunkel. "Scarborough Fair." Lights in all colors joined in with the music, highlighting nothing at first, then showing people in hippie garb dispersed around the room, singing along. They stood still as choir singers until the beat picked up. Then they moved fluidly. I hadn't taken a single sip of my drink, and I had never experienced acid, but this seemed about right for that type of experience.

The tie-dye dancing lights showed enough now that I saw the sparkle in Trey's eyes. His teeth glowed in a beam of black light. His boyish excitement sucked me right into the moment and had my heart beating a little faster. This was a good guy, I had to admit.

The song ended. The room went pitch black again. I snatched for Trey's hand this time.

A circular spotlight popped on. It showed empty space on a small stage. Then the notes for "Mrs. Robinson" started up and a woman's leg appeared, floating in the circle. Her second leg came to meet it, and she crossed one over the other. Her hands came into the light with a cigarette and lighter. When she held the cigarette to her lips to light it, the flare gave us a glimpse of her gorgeous black hair and pale face, and we again only saw the spotlight on her legs and the red tip of the cigarette dangling from her lips. She reached down to the floor and picked up a pair of black stockings. She proceeded to sensually spread them up her legs, taking the entire song to do so. It was oddly enchanting and an incredible turn-on.

The performance continued through a few more songs. Always varying, but continuing to use light and dark to highlight things.

The after party went full on '60s and we left soon after someone lit up a joint and Trey started hacking up a lung.

Back on the street, I supported his weight until he caught his breath.

"Are you asthmatic?" I asked.

"No, I'm fine. Let's find coffee."

We walked on, at a slightly slower pace than usual as Trey had beads of sweat trickling down his forehead.

At an all-night diner, with endless mugs of fresh coffee and a midnight snack of omelets, we talked the night away. Time slipped by, but it didn't matter. Nothing mattered but these moments and that heady feeling you get when getting to know a person you know you really mesh with. I don't remember how many times that night I thought to myself, this guy is my soul mate. He could really be my soul mate.

He took me home. He checked my blood sugar. Then he undressed me and touched me and made me feel like a queen. I swear his bed was made of clouds.

*

The rain dribbled down the glass and woke me the next morning. That, and a shaky feeling and shirt drenched in sweat. The clock showed six a.m.; my meter showed significantly low. I ran to the kitchen—stumbled—and scrounged for sugar. Well supplied with a life-saving glass of juice and biscuits, I started coffee and turned on the telly. News of the upcoming EuroCup and my beloved

German football team was coming in the next segment. I located a mug and poured black coffee, sat on the rug in the living room, and stretched my tired muscles while listening.

"The favored team for winning this year's EuroCup, the Germans, came to Istanbul three weeks ago to prepare," the reporter said. My nose was to my knees, so I didn't see the scene change. "They needn't have bothered though." My head snapped up to see my boys all in hospital beds. "They are all so ill with a mysterious virus they can barely move. They will forfeit their game today and England will move forward."

I jumped up, knocking my coffee over. In the bedroom, I yanked my skirt on and stood with Trey's button-down half buttoned. He was off in bliss land. I couldn't stay. I couldn't do this. I was not allowed happiness. And as long as no one else got hurt, I was okay with that. I would cause no more tragedy. I ran.

chapter 5

I ached. I groaned. I probably looked like a crazy as I stumbled along in the early morning Saturday light, a quiet
time for busy London with few cars splashing through
puddles and red buses emerging from the fog like giant,
friendly beasts. I forced myself to eat a granola bar from
a newsagent and then lost myself in the streets, condensation running down my arms in rivulets like the tears
down my cheeks.

I ended up in my park, among the chipped and tilted
gravestones. The trees created enough cover to send a chill
to my bones. One of the gravestones, far from the path
and draped in ivy, caught my eye, and I plunged through
the undergrowth to reach it. It was plain, square, almost
rusty, but beautiful. What text I saw was a gorgeous,
powerful font. I peeled back the curtain of ivy, shivering
from cold and excitement.

July Fielding
1812-1842

We'll never know her true thoughts,
But we will always love her.

I dropped to my knees. What a breath-taker. Only thirty years old, so beloved, and that name. July. Obvious, simple, stunning.

"She's my favorite," a voice broke the moment, shattered it like glass, and I jumped.

Joe sat on the other side of the grave, leaning against a tree, nearly at one with the forest in his green sweater and tweed flat cap.

"It's a beautiful idea. That they could love her in spite of her secrets, even if she was never fully open. That they could forgive her for being selfish and closed."

"Why do you say selfish?" I asked.

"Because it takes courage to share your deepest self with people, to trust them with your heart."

We sat without speaking. His words reverberated in my head, contradicting everything I had thought about my eerie "gift" up until now. What if I didn't have control over the things I thought I did? What if I wasn't as powerful as I assumed? What if that was arrogant and selfish of me to think that I had that much sway?

But then the image of massacred gorillas passed through my mind. And a future image of Trey's gravestone with only thirty years on the dates.

"No. Sharing all of yourself, burdening those you love, is selfish."

I lifted my gaze to Joe's. A ray of sunshine fell on his face, and he smiled a sad smile.

I stood and walked away. I pulled my phone from my pocket and booked a plane ticket for that afternoon.

*

Sebastian greeted me at the airport in Bratislava with a bear hug that lasted just a little too long. I pushed him away gently and smiled. I hadn't spoken with him since he had left Berlin, and our fling unfinished, until I sent a message saying I was on my way. Ever the good friend, he was at my beck and call.

"Hi!" he said. "Do you want to get some sleep?"

"Let's just get started."

He smirked and grabbed my bag. I squeezed between random building materials for the housing charity he worked for, narrowly avoiding decapitation by some planks of wood while balancing my feet on paint cans.

He took me to a nearly finished build site, plunked heavy cans of paint in my hands, pointed through the doorway, and said "Tschuess!" I watched him drive away with my suitcase and any semblance of company, and I breathed deeply. I then lost myself for hours in gliding a roller on walls with clean paint, in a home meant for someone I didn't know who couldn't be hurt by my love, someone who needed my help and would finally get a break in life, who I could affect positively with no repercussions.

That night, in Sebastian's flat, staring at the ceiling from his sofa, I thought again about Joe's comments. What was really more selfish? Withholding or giving everything to chance?

All night I lay there. Cars occasionally sweeping by in the night, the clock ticking on the wall, the LED from the coffeepot infuriating me. Many subjects meandered through my thoughts though I avoided the one, and any connections to it, that truly required consideration. I finally stood at exactly 4:23—as the pot eagerly informed me. I started the brew and went to stand at the window. I heard footsteps creak on the floorboards and the click of Sebastian's door.

"I'm sorry. Did I wake you?" I said in German.

"Nein."

His arms came around me as he stepped up to cradle me. It felt normal, natural… wrong.

"I missed you," he said.

Apparently, our friendship turned two-week fling before he left Berlin for Slovakia had left an impact. And maybe this was what I needed—someone I liked but didn't love and could be with yet without causing him any pain.

But as I went to run my hands along his forearms, I remembered the chocolatey velvet of Trey's skin. I stopped. I couldn't do this to either of them.

"I'm sorry, Sebastian." I pulled away and went to pour coffee. "This has to stay a friendship."

"There is someone else?" He switched to English, distancing himself from the conversation.

"No. I don't think so. No."

I tested my blood sugar—steady even through the stress. I had control. I glanced at my phone and saw a shit-load of messages. I sent *I'm okay* to Layla and removed all notifications.

Sebastian had taken this reprieve to creep closer and take his cup of coffee, our arms grazing.

"Just for fun?" he whispered, his breath tickling my ear.

I hesitated.

And then berated myself for the hesitation.

"Maybe I should stay with Julia?" The American woman who had made Bratislava her home and had recruited us both for this work in the first place.

"If you want." Sebastian shrugged and then bit into an apple. "We leave for work in an hour," he said as he walked back to his room and closed the door.

*

The bass pounding up through my legs and into my chest cavity drowned out my worries. Bodies rubbed against me, gyrating and flowing and bumping. I lost myself in the music, in the chaos, in the strobe lights. I only allowed myself one drink because the alcohol had negative effects on my blood sugar, and I took all night to drink through it so no one would offer to buy me another.

Sebastian squeezed through the crowd to come up behind me, put his hands on my hips, and sway. I planted a kiss on his lips and smiled. He tasted of liquor and sugar.

We left the club still going strong and made our way to Julia's flat. She welcomed me with open arms and another drink, which I took hesitantly.

"I didn't think I'd ever see you out here," she said. Then she grabbed my hand and pulled me to one of the sofas in her warehouse flat. Someone tinkered on the old piano. In front of the group of sofas, someone stood slamming a poem. Julia tucked her legs beneath her tiny frame and snuggled close so we could whisper.

"Are you here for Sebastian?" she asked.

"God no," I said and chuckled. "I needed to get away."

"From what?"

I stared out of the windows at the moon rising over Bratislava.

"Okay. Don't tell me. But you're here to work on the housing project? That's excellent! My recruiting finally paid off."

I laughed.

"How long will you stay?"

"I don't know. Six months? A year? Whatever works."

"We can always use the help you know. Do you need a room? I know Sebastian is in a one-room, so if you aren't in his bed you'll want more than an Ikea sofa." She winked.

I sighed, relaxing into the cushions. It was good to be around friends again, good to feel like I could let go and not risk hurting these people because I had control over the relationships. I knew where the boundaries lay. This was easier to navigate than my situation with Trey.

Thoughts of him spurred me into action. I jumped up, grabbed Julia's hand, and went over to the sound system where I turned up the music and danced across the expanse. People joined us, including Sebastian, and I tugged him closer to me. It felt like a game of cat and mouse, but I knew I couldn't hurt him so I let myself go, just a little.

*

I lost myself in building homes. So much so that on a day a month after my arrival, one of the locals tapped me on the shoulder and pointed to my phone in my pocket. He grunted and walked away, the others having paused their work to gawk at the wordless exchange.

I had fourteen missed calls. I hadn't heard a single one, but everyone else had. I smiled sheepishly at them as I went outside to sort it out.

It was Layla—thirteen times.

Trey—once.

I called Layla.

"Where the fuck are you!" she squawked shrilly in my ear before it even rang.

"Bratislava," I whispered.

"Do you understand that I haven't slept for a month? Trey called to say you had disappeared after spending the night; he was worried. And then all I get is a measly message saying you're fine. And then nothing. Weeks. Weeks!"

"Okay."

"Piper. You can't run away from your problems."

"You think I don't know that?" I said. "My pancreas is stuck to me, no matter how far I run. Damn organ that doesn't work forcing me to question every single thing I do. Every single day. Forever."

"This is about so much more than you. There are people who actually give a fuck."

"Okay."

She huffed.

"Trey is in the hospital."

"What? Why didn't you start with that? Is it his cough?"

Sebastian emerged from the house into the sunlight. His muscular frame draped in a tool belt looked solid and strong. I wanted to lean on him, but I resisted. He frowned and crossed his arms.

"You need to come home," Layla said, resigned. "That's all I'll say." Then she hung up.

I rang Trey's number—straight to voicemail. I paced and hyperventilated. I texted him *I'm sorry I'm sorry I'm sorry*. Then I dropped to my knees and worried my blood sugar was low from the adrenaline rush but couldn't find the motivation to get food.

A bottle appeared before my eyes. Sebastian held a cola in front of me. I took it, my hand lingering on his in thanks.

"I'll get your things and be back to pick you up," he said.

"You heard?"

"Most."

He walked away, and his car started and rumbled away. Hammering and chatter and birdsong filled my ears. The sun meandered across the sky in a slow march. Finally, the car returned and I stepped inside.

chapter 6

Antiseptic. Squeaky linoleum. Beeping monitors. The memory of scratchy linens and the vacuum of time when Layla told me my parents had died. A wave of water tumbling over me, silencing my surroundings.

And now I stood before a window looking in at a patient asleep on a bed. This patient was not a child and did not have a disease that could be lived with.

Cancer. Stage four. It echoed in my ears. More bad news Layla had delivered with her honey-laced voice. I swayed. Her arm came up around me. She pulled me away and led me to the cafe. We sat. We stared. We sipped.

"I haven't known him that long," I said.

"Time is a fickle mistress."

"But how can I love him? How can I be affecting him like this? Why can't I get my happiness under control? Why am I even here?" That last I screamed and shoved my chair back with a screech. Layla simply lifted her head to me.

"Go talk to him," she whispered. "Just because you barely know him doesn't mean you can't love him. And love means losing control."

I gawped at her.

I had come so close to telling her, to revealing my magic. The one person left in my life I had managed to save from disaster and I had nearly thrown all that hard work away.

She didn't know. I would never tell her. I walked away, shielding my heart from her scrutiny.

Upstairs I stayed on the safe side of the glass a little longer. Trey stirred, his rail-thin body barely lifting the blankets, and turned to see me. He smiled.

Inside the room smelled of oxygen and purifiers. No flowers were allowed. No perfumes or strong scents. Nothing that could irritate his barely-there lungs.

"I'm sorry," I said. My arms hung limp. I couldn't bring myself to sit in the available chair or move a step closer than the center of the room. Space yawned away from me, making the gap seem even broader.

"Not much you can do. No need to be sorry." He coughed.

"I meant for leaving."

"Oh. That. I guess I should be mad, but under the circumstances." He took a deep, rattling breath. "Are you all right? Did I do something?"

At those words, I jumped the chasm and landed next to him. My hand found his.

"No. It's not you; it's me."

We laughed. He hacked.

"I'm here now," I said. "I'll be here."

"Until I die," he finished my statement and the world closed in on us.

*

Spoon feed him soup.

Pray he doesn't vomit it all back into the kidney-shaped bowl.

Read the Sunday comics, on a Thursday, to him because his eyes have failed after all of the medicine.

Try to laugh even though I don't hear the jokes my own voice says.

Realize his laughs are also fake.

Put the paper down.

Pick up the TV remote.

Take a sip of water.

Hold the cup and straw to his lips.

Watch TV until I remember he can barely see and is gazing into the sunlight.

"Don't go toward the light," I say.

He chuckles.

And coughs.

And spits up blood.

And moans.

Drag my ass to the hospital every day.

Force myself to be present.

Remind myself it's not my fault.

Test my blood sugar.

Fall more in love with someone than I ever have before.

Test my blood sugar.

Keep the tears in check.

Sit quietly while Layla waxes lyrical about our trip to Tower Bridge. But in all honesty, her visit did more for him in an hour than I have managed in a week.

Read *Wuthering Heights* aloud until I realize how depressing classic literature is—pull out the comics again.

Stroke his skin to give him some semblance of pleasure among the pain.

Pinch myself to give myself some semblance of pain among the pain.

Watch from outside the window while the doctors attempt to get his convulsing body to accept and utilize oxygen again.

Step foot inside the room only to find an invisible barrier blocking my entrance.

Realize I love this man too much.

Realize I can't do this anymore.

Realize I'm running away, again.

chapter 7

I would love to say that I forgot. That my curse no longer affected Trey. That I went back to being sad, angry, lonely, and that Trey healed and went on to live a long, full life.

But the curse had taken hold. I had loved him too long and fate could not be reversed. He would die, whether I was there or not.

I spent only a week in misery before returning to my torture chamber with my tail between my legs. A week of sitting on benches, sitting in coffee houses, sitting on curbs. I saw people. So many people. Some were happy—like a young family walking in Hyde Park, or an old couple hobbling onto the Tube for an adventure. Some, not so much.

It didn't matter how much I blinked. The scene before me moved along like a stop motion, but the timeline was not altered. Neither in my physical world nor in my soul. Trey still commandeered my thoughts.

I had to go back.

So, I did.

And what I found was a breathing corpse.

As I went through the doorway, a nurse squeezed my shoulder. Layla smiled from the chair by his bed. Trey rolled to see who she saw. Then he rolled away again. I deserved that.

Layla left after kissing his cheek, and I took her place. His eyes never focused on me.

We sat as the sun set behind me. We sat through the staff change. Finally, his hand crept across the bed to find mine.

Something suddenly occurred to me.

"Where is your family?"

His eyes found mine and swam in the depths.

"I don't have any."

"Friends?" I whispered.

"Cancer and friends don't good bedfellows make. Didn't you wonder why I never told you?"

I shrugged.

"What about you?"

I crawled onto the bed with him.

"Parents are dead. My fault." The words eked out like cough syrup in reverse. Had I really just said that?

"What happened?"

"I blinked." My sobs should have shook the world, but they barely shook the bed. Was I telling him because I knew my secret would go to his grave? No. I was telling him so he knew why he was going to his grave.

He didn't say more. His patience seemed limitless. But the words turned from mud to water.

"I'm cursed. Whenever I am happy, content with life, those I love get hurt. It started when I was very young. And when I was ten, I was diagnosed with Type 1. A few days after diagnosis I found a way to accept my fate. And at that exact moment, my parents' car flew off a bridge."

I paused to wipe away the snot and tears.

"I've kept it in check, with minimal disasters. I even managed a relationship with Layla, and a fling or two, with barely a paper cut. Until I met you."

I looked into his brown eyes.

"And now I'm killing you."

For a moment, confusion filtered through the fog. He had burst out laughing. He was laughing at me, at my pain. I catapulted from the bed.

"I'm sorry," he said through the tears and hiccups and coughs. "Come back. Please." He didn't even have the strength to motion with his hand.

I sat on the edge of the bed, hugging my knees.

"I'm not laughing at you," he said. I waited while he caught what breath he could. "I'm laughing that you think my cancer could be your fault. Was my skin cancer before I met you your fault? I had the lung cancer before we met. So it's ridiculous."

"But it always correlates," I said.

"Possible. But correlation does not equal causation." He waited until I looked up. "You can't control life."

"Or death."

"Don't be morbid," he snapped. "You can't go on like this. I refuse to leave until you tell me this isn't your fault. You want me to continue in agony? Or will you let me, and this, go?"

My hands started shaking. I was sweaty and cold. A tension headache prodded my brain from the left. I stood to find my test kit. As I poked my finger, drew blood, awaited the result I knew in my gut would be low, I said, "My entire life is control. I depend upon control. I would die without it."

I measured out an exact amount of sugar tablets and popped one in my mouth.

"Control inherently allows for letting go," he said. He put the effort in and opened his arms. I went to him. "Yes, you need to stay healthy, but you will never reach perfection. It's your flaws I love the most. I love that I need to take care of your diabetes. I love this scar on your nose." He touched it. "But I don't love the idea of you living your life in misery to potentially save others. You'll save others by loving them, by being there for them."

I missed my parents. Even before they had died I had known my happiness held a dark magic. But maybe, just maybe, I could figure out a way to live with that magic. I could let it go by letting it take over. I could revoke its power by accepting it.

"No promises," I said.

"I only ask that you try," he said.

"Okay," I whispered.

"Okay," he said.

And then we slept. Him wheezing; me sniffling. Wrapped in and around and through each other, melded as one while the world spun around us.

As the sun rose and pulled me from my slumber, I felt free. Even when I found my arms enveloping a still and empty body, I felt strong.

acknowledgements

There can never be the right words to express my gratitude. Thank you to my Type 1 diabetes for inspiring me in so many ways and challenging me each and every day. (I also hate you, is there a place I can write that part down?)

Thank you to my beta readers (Janet, Shanthi, Debbie, and Julie). You helped me find some glaring errors and bolstered my courage.

Thank you to my editor, Ellen Bollman, for the excellent lesson on how to make my writing—here and in future—stronger. I will forever use "by a zombie" at the end of a passive sentence.

Thank you to my husband for the constant support and my son for the days ambling around in the sunshine discovering new things.

about the author

Amie McCracken is an imaginist. Her stories dive deep into the what-ifs of life. Swimming in books her whole life, her career as an editor and book designer was only natural. She hails from the US of A but has lived abroad for most of her adult life. With a book or three on her nightstand, a manuscript in progress on her laptop, and a cup of tea to hand, Amie is a storyteller.

Find out more about her at amiemccrackenauthor.com.

If you liked this book, please help other readers find it by posting a review

If you would like to find out more about Amie McCracken, visit her website amiemccrackenauthor.com

If you would like to connect with Amie sign up for her newsletter at amiemccracken.com/newsletter